JONAH AND THE WHALE

Based on a traditional retelling from the Bible by Denny Kaltreider

Illustrated By
Kristine Marsh

Jonah and the Whale
Text and Illustrations Copyright 2016 by Black Jacket Media, LLC. Logo and all related characters are Registered Trademarks of Black Jacket Media, LLC.
All rights reserved. Printed in the United States of America. No part of this book may be used or reproduced in any manner whatsoever
without written permission except in the case of brief quotations embodied in critical articles and reviews.
Black Jacket Media, LLC, 2020 Fieldstone Parkway, Suite 200-954, Franklin, TN 37069 - www.blackjacket.media

One day in a town near Nazareth,
the sun was high in the sky. The Lord spoke
to Jonah and asked him to go to Nineveh.
The Lord wanted the people of Nineveh to
change their wicked ways.

But Jonah didn't want to go to Nineveh,
so he ran in the opposite direction
toward the seaport of Joppa.

He bought a ticket for a trip aboard a ship going to Tarshish. He thought he would be able to hide there from the Lord.

But the Lord knew what Jonah was doing,
so he sent a terrible storm. It rocked the
ship back and forth, up and down,
and threatened to sink it.

All the sailors on board were very frightened. They threw some of the cargo into the sea to lighten the ship.

Jonah had gone below deck and had fallen into a deep sleep. The captain woke him up.

"How can you sleep?"
he said.

"Get up and call on your god!
Maybe he will take notice of us,
and we will not perish."

Then the sailors found out
that the storm had come
because of Jonah.

So the sailors asked him,

"Tell us, what is responsible
for making this trouble for us?
Where do you come from?
What is your country?
What kind of person are you?"

Jonah told them,

"I am a Hebrew and I
worship the Lord,
the God of heaven,
who made the sea and the land."

The sailors actually knew by now
Jonah was running away from the Lord.

They asked him,
"What have you done?"

14

All the while, the sea kept getting
rougher and rougher.

"What can we do to make the
sea calm down?"

"Pick me up and throw me into the sea,"
he replied,

"and it will become calm. I know it is my fault that this great storm has come upon you."

Instead, the sailors tried to row back to land.
But as hard as they tried, they simply could not
get the boat back to shore because the
sea grew even wilder than before.

**Then they took Jonah and threw him overboard.
The raging sea grew calm.**

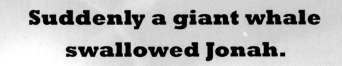

Suddenly a giant whale swallowed Jonah.

19

20

While inside the whale,
Jonah prayed for three days
and three nights. He recounted
how he had run away
from the Lord's Word and how he
was thrown into the sea.

Jonah also vowed that if he were spared,
he would change his ways and
do what the Lord asked.

"Salvation comes from the Lord,"
he prayed.

When he heard Jonah's plea,
the Lord made the whale
spit Jonah out onto dry land.

He spoke to Jonah and asked him
for the second time to go to Nineveh
and give the people there his message.

26

This time Jonah obeyed the Lord's command and he went and shared the message with the people of Nineveh.

The people believed the message
and changed their ways.
And the Lord was pleased.

For more fun visit
StoryChimes.net

67643385R00020

Made in the USA
Lexington, KY
17 September 2017